50000

CU00900680

Metropolitan
Borough of Wirral
Schools' Library Service

0151 346 1184

Wirral Education Centre, Acre Lane,
Bromborough, Wirral.

16 DEC 1998

18 MAR 1999

Wirral
Schools
Library
Service

Forbidden Ground

Elizabeth Laird

Forbidden Ground

DH OF WIRRAL
SURE SERVICES
ARTS

METROPOLITAN BOROUGH
DEPARTMENT OF WIRRAL
LIBRARIES AND

WITHDRAWN FROM STOCK

Hamïsh Hamilton • London

HAMISH HAMILTON

Published by the Penguin Group
Penguin Books Ltd, 27 Wrights Lane, London w8 5tz, England
Penguin Books USA Inc., 375 Hudson Street, New York, New York 10014, USA
Penguin Books Australia Ltd, Ringwood, Victoria, Australia
Penguin Books Canada Ltd, 10 Alcorn Avenue, Toronto, Ontario, Canada m4v 3b2
Penguin Books (NZ) Ltd, 182–190 Wairau Road, Auckland 10, New Zealand

Penguin Books Ltd, Registered Offices: Harmondsworth, Middlesex, England

First published 1997
1 3 5 7 9 10 8 6 4 2

Copyright © Elizabeth Laird, 1997

The moral right of the author has been asserted

Set in 12/18pt Monotype Palatino
Typeset by Rowland Phototypesetting Ltd,
Bury St Edmunds, Suffolk
Printed in England by Clays Ltd, St Ives plc

All rights reserved.
Without limiting the rights under copyright reserved above, no part of this
publication may be reproduced, stored in or introduced into a retrieval
system, or transmitted, in any form or by any means (electronic, mechanical,
photocopying, recording or otherwise), without the prior written permission
of both the copyright owner and the above publisher of this book.

British Library Cataloguing in Publication Data
A CIP catalogue record for this book is available from the British Library

ISBN 0-241-13763-2

METROPOLITAN BOROUGH
OF WIRRAL
DEPT. OF LEISURE SERVICES
LIBRARIES AND ARTS DIVISION

SBN	S739556	
ACC.N		
LOAN COPY		Y.P.
CLASS No.	TEEN	

CHAPTER ONE

'I'm not having it, Hannah,' said Mrs Rasi. 'I'm not having you go out in the street like a no-good girl from an American film.'

She stabbed the point of her hot iron at the creases in her husband's shirt, ignoring Susu, who was crying and pulling at the hem of her dress. Hannah stared at her mother, not sure if it was worth trying to argue or not.

'I'll be the only one in the whole school,' she said, picking up Susu to stop the noise. 'All the others wear their skirts much shorter than this. They laugh at me, Mum. They say I'm . . .'

'You think I care what they say?' Mrs Rasi

1

took Susu out of her arms and put him over her shoulder. Her hand went automatically to the smooth curve of his back and she began to pat him in a comforting rhythm. 'Showing your legs right up to the knee! What sort of girl are you? And your blouse . . .'

'OK, OK,' said Hannah. She'd lost the battle of the hemline, for the time being anyway. She couldn't face the thought of another battle over her short-sleeved blouse. She pulled the skirt down from the waistband, over which she had so carefully tucked it.

'A bit better, I suppose,' Mrs Rasi said, 'but it's still . . .'

'I don't believe it!' Hannah pretended to notice the clock on the shelf by the door for the first time. 'Eight o'clock! I'll miss the bus!' and she picked up her schoolbag and ran out of the house.

'You hitch it up again and I'll get your father on to you!' Mrs Rasi called after her, but Susu had fallen asleep on her shoulder and she had to speak too softly for Hannah to hear.

'Indecent,' whispered Mrs Rasi. She went over to

the bed in the corner of the room, pulled back the bright red cotton coverlet and laid the sleeping baby down. 'If I'd shown my legs like that when I was fifteen, my mother would have taken a strap to me. Quite right too.'

Susu whimpered and snuffled in his sleep. His cheek was red where a new tooth was coming through. He'd been fretting for days. Mrs Rasi went over to the stove and began to heat some milk. She had enough to worry about, with a difficult baby and little Karim and Farida under her feet all day. She couldn't waste more time worrying about Hannah.

The girls stood in a knot at the bus stop, their school books clasped in their arms. Their heads were together, bright headscarves almost touching, and their hands were held up to their mouths, covering giggles, as they pored over a piece of paper that Zahra was holding.

Where do you get confidence from? thought Hannah, her heart sinking. Her eyes on the girls, she nearly walked into a man who was squatting on the pavement under a palm tree, sheltering his eyes from the bright North African sun.

Clumsy, stupid, pathetic, that's me.

She sized up Zahra's jeans and smart jacket. They were unbearably fashionable. Sickeningly stylish. Hannah tried to hitch her skirt up again, but she couldn't see to get it straight without a mirror and she was hampered by her bag. Worse if it hangs down all uneven, she thought, and tugged at it again.

Zahra looked up and saw her coming. She whispered to the girl beside her, who looked up too and rolled her eyes, laughing out loud. Zahra slipped the paper back into her bag.

'Oh, hi,' said Hannah, trying to smile and sounding as casual as she could. 'What's the big joke then?'

'It's nothing.' Zahra flicked the ends of her scarf back over her shoulders. 'You wouldn't think it was funny, anyway.'

'Go on. Try me.'

Here it was. Another test. If she failed it, like she'd failed all the others, she'd be out on her own, just as she had been every single day since she'd started at this huge city school.

4

Zahra pulled the paper out of her bag again and put it into Hannah's hand. It was a photograph, cut out of a European magazine, and it showed Sylvester Stallone lying beside a swimming pool, showing more of himself than he'd probably intended.

Hannah had never seen anything like it before.

'Look at her blushing!' one of the other girls said. 'She's all embarrassed! Doesn't know where to look!'

The others said nothing. They were watching her.

'Wow!' said Hannah, making herself laugh. 'What a hunk, eh?'

The bus came. The girls crowded on to it. Hannah knew, when Zahra looked at her, that she'd passed the test.

'Come and sit here, by me,' said Zahra, patting the empty seat beside her, and Hannah sank down into it, swinging her bag on to her lap in the jaunty way that Zahra did it.

'We're going for a walk after school,' Zahra said. 'Want to come?'

'I'd love to.' Hannah reached into her bag, pulled

out a tube of sweets and offered one to Zahra.

I've got all day, she thought, to think up a story for Mum. Trouble with the bus would do it. She never goes further than the next street. The buses are all a mystery to her.

CHAPTER TWO

Zahra sat beside Hannah in the maths lesson later that morning and let her use her beautiful white ruler. Then, during break, Muna loosened Hannah's hair from the tight little band that held it at the back of her head and teased it out over her shoulders.

'Not bad,' she said, standing back to look, her head on one side. 'It's good the way it hangs down, kind of straight and heavy. Wish mine did.'

When the last bell sounded and the girls streamed out of the metal school gates, Hannah was, for the first time, one of a group of friends.

'Are we going down to the Bab el Jenna as usual?' said Fatima.

'Yeah,' Zahra said. She turned to Hannah. 'Have you been there? That gateway in the old city wall on the way to the central mosque?'

Hannah shook her head. Zahra nudged Muna.

'We'll show her, eh? You'll like it, Hannah. There's a food stall. Cold drinks. Snacks.'

Hanna saw Muna wink at Fatima and she looked away, worried.

'I can't stay long,' she said. 'My mum'll kill me if I'm late.'

'Mine kills me every day,' said Zahra, 'and would you believe it, I'm still alive.'

'Yes, well, she needs me really. To help with Karim and Farida. Especially now. My little brother's teething.'

'Five minutes,' said Zahra. 'That's all it'll be. Just a little walk. No harm in it.'

They'd been going quite fast and the central mosque's gilded minaret was in sight. They were walking along beside the high wall of the old city. Trees from the wilderness inside stood up above its ancient orange brick walls which were topped with pointed battlements. Set into the wall was the medieval Bab el Jenna, the Paradise Gate, and out-side it two tourist guides and a souvenir seller waited, looking up at everything that approached, including a stray dog, hoping for tourists.

'It's very nice here,' said Hannah, feeling puzzled, and looking round at the bare beaten earth, the litter that had blown up against the wall and the food stall owner's flea bitten donkey. 'But don't you like going down the main street, where the shops are?'

'No. We like it here.' Zahra wasn't looking at Hannah. She kept turning her head sideways to look down the road. 'The stall's over there. It's not bad. You can get a Pepsi and they've got sweets too.'

Hannah's hand crept into her pocket and closed round the only coin in it, which was just enough to pay the bus fare home.

'I'm not hungry,' she said. 'Maybe later.'

Zahra suddenly tossed her head, grabbed Fatima and Muna by their arms and began to walk away from the old gate, back towards the town.

'Where are you going?' said Hannah, hurrying to

keep up with them. 'Did I say anything? I didn't mean . . .'

Then she heard feet pounding along behind her and she turned to see a group of four or five young men racing up to them.

'Hi, Zahra!' one of them was shouting, over the whoops and laughs of the others.

'Don't look at them!' hissed Zahra. 'Pretend you haven't seen them!'

Hannah hardly had time to turn round again and walk on beside Zahra when the young men were upon them. They ran round to the front, blocking the girls' way. Hannah's heart, which had begun to beat fast with fright, slowed down again. They were not men, but boys, around seventeen or eighteen years old. And they looked friendly, not threatening at all.

'Zahra! What's the matter with you?' said the oldest-looking boy. 'Don't you like me any more?'

Zahra turned her head away from him and raised her eyebrows to make herself look proud and offended. Muna and Fatima giggled and nudged each other.

'Come on,' the boy said. 'Come back to the stall. I'll get you a Pepsi. OK, so you don't want a Pepsi? A Fanta! A Seven-up!'

Zahra was still walking, but she was beginning to slow down.

'Don't think I'm going to speak to you, Omer,' she said. 'Because I'm not.'

He smacked his hand against his forehead.

'Why? Why on earth?'

'You know why,' she said, looking severe.

'I don't!' the boy protested. 'You're such a tease, Zahra. I never know with you. I never know where I am.'

Hannah looked from Zahra to Omer. Their talk confused her. She couldn't understand what Omer was supposed to have done and why, if Zahra was offended, she had slowed right down and was letting Omer take her bag and carry it for her. But then she jumped as a voice spoke at her elbow.

'Hello.'

She turned. A tall boy was smiling at her. She only had the courage to take one quick sideways

11

look at him, but she saw that his black hair was straight and thick and that it jutted out boldly above his square forehead.

'What's your name?' he said.

'Hannah,' mumbled Hannah, too quietly for him to hear. She knew her face was going red and she bent her head to hide it.

'Hannah,' she said again, a little louder.

She'd never talked to a boy before, except for her cousins in the village. This person was a strange being to her, and it felt as peculiar talking to him as if he'd been a camel or a hippopotamus.

If anyone sees this and tells Mum, I'm done for, she thought.

Guilt and nervousness made her stumble. The boy put his hand out and grasped her elbow to steady her. Then he dropped his hand again.

'I'm Sami,' he said. 'I'm sure I've never met you. You haven't come here before with Zahra and the others, have you?'

'No,' muttered Hannah.

'That's good,' the boy said. 'I mean, look at them, all this silly teasing and pretending to be offended and never saying what they mean. You don't look like them. You're a – oh, I don't know – a real person.'

Hannah dared to glance at him again. Sami wasn't looking at her. He was staring straight ahead and his face looked serious.

'I haven't lived here long,' she said, feeling a little braver. 'My family comes from a village up in the north. We only moved to the city a couple of months ago.'

'That's an incredible coincidence!' Sami said. 'I only came last July! From the south. Do you like it here?'

'Some things are OK.' Hannah sounded doubtful. 'But I haven't made any real friends yet. Not like my old friends at home.'

'I *hate* it!' Sami kicked out at an empty drink can and sent it flying. It crashed against the old wall. 'I only stick it because I want to go to school and there isn't one in my village. My family's at home. I mean my parents and my brothers and everyone. I'm living with my uncle.'

Hannah nodded.

'People think you're a fool because you haven't seen all the films.'

'And they laugh at you because you don't know all the words to the pop songs.'

They turned and looked at each other. Hannah was the first to look away.

'The girls are different here,' she said. 'They're allowed to go out all the time and do what they like. It's as if they're not Muslims at all. My mum's so strict. I mean, she never lets me . . .'

It occurred to her that he might think she was as bad as the rest.

'I only came with them today because I'm sick of them laughing at me,' she said. 'I thought we were just going round the shops. I didn't realize they'd come to meet . . .'

She stopped, embarrassed. He didn't seem to notice anything strange. He was smiling at her.

'Your mum's right, really,' he said. 'I mean, she's your mother. She doesn't want you to go off with some wicked, deceiving man and get yourself into trouble.'

He pulled his collar up and waggled his

eyebrows, trying to look sinister and devious. Hannah laughed. He's just kind and funny, she thought. Funny and nice.

Without realizing it, they'd moved ahead of the others. Hannah looked round and saw that Zahra and Omer and the rest of them had turned back towards the gate. They were at the snack stall, buying drinks.

'I must go home,' said Hannah, feeling nervous again.

'Yes,' said Sami. 'Me too. Come again tomorrow. Please come.'

Hannah stirred a little mound of dust with the toe of her shoe.

'I don't know,' she said. 'I might.'

'Please,' said Sami again. 'I'm not like the others. I don't just think about being with a girl. I really like you. I want us to be friends.'

Hannah felt a glowing warmth, although the sun had gone in and the spring day was cool.

'I'll see,' she said. 'I'll try.' And without a backward glance at Zahra and the others, she began to run home.

CHAPTER THREE

Hannah was at the bus stop early the next morning. She'd been up almost since dawn and had washed her hair and secretly used on her face some of the precious cream that her father had given her mother when Susu was born. Her skin felt different, soft and a little waxy.

'There, you see?' said Zahra, arriving at the bus stop and causing, as she always did, a flutter of attention from the crowd of people waiting for the bus. 'You're still alive! Did your mum try to kill you? Did your dad beat you black and blue?'

'No, actually,' said Hannah. 'No one even noticed I was late. My little brother was crying all day.

Mum was too shattered to think about anything else.'

'I told you,' said Zahra. 'Coming again today?'

'Yeah, I might as well.' Hannah spoke as casually as she could.

'That boy, the tall one who talked to you all the time,' said Zahra, looking without blinking into Hannah's face, her fingers fiddling with the tasselled edge of her scarf, 'he really liked you. I could tell.'

Hannah felt her cheeks go hot.

'He didn't. It wasn't like that. It's just that he's new here, like me.'

She saw with relief that the bus was coming.

'Where is everyone?' she said. 'They'll be late.'

'Who cares?' said Zahra, pushing forward to climb on to the bus.

The morning dragged by slowly. Hannah couldn't keep her eyes on her books or her mind on the teacher's droning voice. She had a strange feeling in her stomach, as if sweet and sour things were curdling in it, and she didn't know if she was glad or sorry when the final bell went.

Zahra linked arms with her as they went out

through the gates and Fatima and Muna followed on behind.

'What's Omer's family like?' said Hannah, thinking about Sami.

Zahra stared at her.

'His *family*? I've got no idea. What do you want to know that for?'

'Oh, no reason.' Hannah chewed on her lip.

'Omer and me, it's got nothing to do with families. It's just a bit of fun.'

They turned the last corner. The old gate was in view now.

He won't come, thought Hannah. I know he won't come.

'Bet Hannah gets all excited when she sees her boyfriend,' Fatima called out from behind.

Muna giggled.

'Bet she does! She practically ran all the way here. Look at me, I'm out of breath trying to keep up.'

Hannah slowed down at once.

'You're too fat, Muna, that's your trouble,' said Zahra over her shoulder. 'You couldn't run if an axeman was after you.'

18

There was a shout from behind and they all turned round. Omer and his friends were running up to them, just as they had done the day before. Hannah felt an odd kicking sensation in her stomach, but it stopped almost at once. Sami wasn't there. He hadn't come.

Zahra, Fatima and Muna were walking on, pretending to annoy the boys, but Hannah's feet felt leaden. She fell behind.

Stupid! Stupid! she told herself. Why am I so stupid?

The crowd of boys reached her, parted to move round her and passed on after the other girls.

Hannah trailed behind them awkwardly.

I could slip off now and they wouldn't notice, she thought. They wouldn't have the chance to tease me.

Then, out of the corner of her eye, she saw something move under the arch of the Paradise Gate. Someone in a white shirt was standing in the deep shadows. A hand was waving to her. Signalling. Beckoning. Hannah hesitated. The person stepped out of the greyness into the bright sunshine. She recognized him with a shock of joy. It was Sami.

He was waving to her again. She nodded her head towards him and he moved back into the shadows.

She felt bold and confident. She ran up to Zahra and touched her arm.

'I'm going home,' she said. 'See you tomorrow. I promised Mum I wouldn't be too late.'

Zahra hardly heard her.

'Oh sure,' she said. 'See you.'

Hannah walked back along the old wall until she came to the gate. She looked round. The others seemed to have forgotten her. They were doubled over with laughter at something one of the boys had said. Hannah slipped through the old arched gateway and came face to face at once with Sami.

He'd been leaning against the wall, trying to look casual. She couldn't look straight into his face, but focused on the rich brown colour of his neck where it met the white collar of his shirt.

'Hi,' he said.

His voice squeaked a little and he had to cough to clear his throat.

'Hi,' she said.

He was looking down at her and she felt a distracting buzzing in her ears. She glanced up into his eyes once or twice but felt too embarrassed to stare right back at him. Instead, she turned away and looked down over the tops of the trees.

'What is this place?' she said.

'It's the old city.' He was glad of something to say. 'No one's lived here since the Romans.'

The place was like a vast walled garden that spilled down the hillside towards the river in the valley below. From the high point by the gate where they were standing, a tapestry of trees fell away below them. There were pale-leaved oleanders, fluffy mimosas, the dark tall spikes of cypresses and orange and lemon trees covered with bright fruit.

'It's all open below the trees,' said Sami. 'You can see the old walls, where the houses and streets were. It's brilliant. Come on.'

He started off along the broad path that led down through the trees. Hannah held back. The garden was quiet. The branches trembled in the light spring breeze, but no human movement was there. The shimmering leaves, golden fruit and crumbling walls appeared to watch and wait for something to happen. Hannah needed to feel brave to go on down the hill. She wasn't afraid of Sami, who had stopped and was looking at her, a question in his serious brown eyes, but of herself. She might change. She might feel things and learn things that would frighten her if she went any further.

A gardener stepped out from between the trees, walking up the hill with a bucket in his hand. He said nothing and scarcely glanced at them. Hannah was reassured.

People like us often come here then, she thought. It's all right.

Sami watched her as she stood still, not knowing what to do. He looked hurt.

'Are you scared?' he said. 'I'm not going to touch you. I only want to show you something.'

'I'm not scared of *you*,' she said quickly. 'It's this place. It's . . . I'll come down a little way.'

Side by side they began to walk down the path.

'I've thought about you all the time, every minute, since yesterday,' Sami said, and his voice was strained as if he had a lump in his throat.

She couldn't hide her delighted smile. He saw it and knew she'd been thinking of him too. He took her hand. His fingers felt strong, and she felt the glow of his touch creep up her arm.

'I know you'll think I'm mad,' he went on, laughing a little nervously, 'but I've got this weird feeling, really strange, that we feel the same way about everything. You know, that we like the same things, think about the same things . . .'

There were wild flowers under the trees, a bright mass of pink and yellow dotting the vivid green. Her eyes were on them, but she didn't see them. She was only aware of Sami. She could see with her side vision the way his cotton sleeve moved as his arm swung, the way his head turned, how he reached up to hold a low branch out of her way. She didn't need to look directly at him to guess the expression on his face. It would be intense and surprised, like hers.

'Yes,' she said. 'Yes. I feel it too.'

'We'll try it out!' he said. 'What's your favourite colour?'

She felt safe and very happy.

'Oh, blue, you know, that really greeny kind of blue.'

'There! You see? It's mine too! Blue's always been mine. And music – what sort of music do you like?'

'I – I'm not sure,' she said, feeling a little anxious now in case she said something silly or naive. 'I know everyone likes pop –' She shot a sidelong glance at him. His face gave nothing away. 'I mean, I think it's wonderful and everything . . .'

'Do you?' he sounded disappointed.

'Yes, well, I mean, everyone says it's wonderful so I suppose it must be.' She paused and gathered up her courage. 'But I really like Cheb Khaled.'

'Yes!' He punched the air with his free hand. 'I *knew* you'd say that! Just like yesterday, I knew you'd say you hadn't been here long and that the others weren't your real friends. I could tell you were different. Special.'

They'd been going down some broad steps and had come out from under the trees on to a terrace paved with blocks of worn stone. They could look down from here into the lower part of the huge walled enclosure.

'Look,' said Sami. 'Down there.'

A tumble of ruins lay below, their broken brown walls sticking up out of the thick spring weeds that had sprouted, green and lush, between the old stones. At one corner was a clump of gnarled trees, their twisted roots gripping the earth like old hands, and beside them, a single finger pointing to the sky, was a broken minaret. There were still traces of the turquoise and lapis lazuli tiles that had once covered its surface centuries ago, although most of them had crumbled away. Now the bare brick underneath was scoured and gouged by wind and rain.

On top of the minaret, a pair of storks had built a messy nest of sticks and twigs. One of them was standing on it. He was clacking his beak and rolling his head back towards his tail. The sound, like pieces of wood being beaten against each other, echoed round the deserted garden.

Hannah burst out laughing.

'Storks!' she said. 'Was that what you wanted me to see? It's just like home! We've always got them nesting in our village. We used to have some on our roof. I love them. They're kind of crazy and beautiful at the same time.'

The storks made her happier than anything else.

The stork's mate was flying towards the nest now, her long red legs dangling, her black-tipped wings curling a little at the tips. She landed clumsily and the male bobbed his head at her, up and down, up and down, and clattered his beak enthusiastically.

'They make you dream of flying,' said Sami. 'Maybe these very ones flew here from home. Yours or mine.'

The word 'home' made Hannah gasp.

'I've got to go! My mum'll be going out of her mind!'

She turned and began to run back up the steps. Sami ran after her and caught her arm.

'Wait!' he said. 'Just one more moment. I've got to tell you. Something's happening to me. I felt it yesterday, but a hundred times more today. I've never known anything like this in my life before.'

She felt solemn, in spite of the happiness bursting inside her.

'Me too,' she said. 'I feel it too.'

'Come on! Let's run!'

He began to leap up the steps, and she raced after him, feeling that her feet were so light they might at any moment leave the ground.

They stopped, panting and laughing, just inside the Paradise Gate.

'We only met yesterday,' said Hannah. 'We hardly know each other.'

'Oh, but we do!' Sami shook his thatch of dark hair away from his eyes. 'I feel like I've never known anyone so well in the whole of my life.'

She smiled at him, knowing that everything she felt was in her face for him to read, and that she needn't bother to hide it.

'You'll be here tomorrow, won't you?' she said.

'Tomorrow, and every day. I promise.'

Chapter Four

'Hannah, where have you *been*?'

Mrs Rasi stood at the open door. The baby, his black curls damp and tousled, lay on her shoulder, his eyes half closed.

'Sorry, Mum,' panted Hannah. 'It was the bus. It – broke down.'

Susu whimpered. Mrs Rasi jiggled him gently.

'Just when I needed you most! Look at him! Look at Susu! He's been on and on, crying like this all day.'

Hannah looked at the baby. His cheeks were flushed and he was breathing rapidly through half-open lips.

'He's only teething, isn't he?' she said. She wasn't used to illness. None of them had ever had anything worse than a cold.

'Well, that's just it! I don't know what it is! Mrs Rehab from over the road popped in this morning because she heard him crying so much and she thinks he's got something. She reckoned it might be pneumonia!' Mrs Rasi touched Susu's forehead. 'Look at him, all hot and miserable! And he won't even lift his head properly. None of you were ever like this when you were teething.'

Hannah felt frightened.

'You'd better take him to a doctor, Mum.'

'A doctor?' Anxiety drove Mrs Rasi's voice up a pitch. 'Where am I going to find a doctor?'

'We could ask Mrs Rehab.' Hannah stroked one of Susu's small brown feet but he pulled it up out of her reach and began to cry again.

'She doesn't know any doctors. All she said was to take him to that clinic place next to the garage on the main road. I don't know anything about them! I don't know how much they'll cost or even if they'll let me in!'

Susu began to shiver.

'He looks terrible, Mum,' said Hannah. 'You'd better take him. I'll come with you.'

'No.' Mrs Rasi picked up her purse and put it in her pocket. 'You stay here with Farida and Karim. Oh God, I wish we were at home!'

She tucked a blanket round Susu and put on her shoes. At the door she turned back.

'Your father ought to be back by six. Tell him I'm at the clinic. Tell him to come.'

She shut the door behind her and the bright patch of sunlight on the stone floor of the dark little living room disappeared. Hannah felt the change inside her. Sami and the storks and her brilliant happiness fell away and guilt and anxiety crept in on her.

'I want a biscuit! Get me a biscuit!' said Karim, running up to her on fat little legs.

'Mummy said he wasn't to have any more,' said Farida, looking up at Hannah over the blanket she was carefully folding to make a bed for her doll.

Susu's bound to be all right. Mum's just panicking, thought Hannah. Nothing can go wrong today.

She felt so sure of it that she was no longer

anxious. She fetched the biscuit tin down from the high shelf above the cooker.

'Only one,' she said to Karim, 'and if you go on making a fuss I won't do you anything nice for supper.'

The afternoon settled into its rhythm. Hannah cooked the supper and finished the ironing and kept an eye on the children. Every now and then she caught herself humming a tune by Cheb Khaled, and when she went past the small mirror that hung over the little basin where her father shaved, she saw that she was smiling.

Mr Rasi came home at the usual time. He kicked off his shoes by the door and started taking off his jacket.

'Daddy, Daddee!' shouted Karim, clasping his father's leg below the knee.

Mr Rasi gently detached him and went to the basin to wash his face and hands.

'Mum's taken Susu to the clinic,' said Hannah, handing him a towel. 'Mrs Rehab thinks he might have pneumonia.'

As she spoke she felt horribly afraid.

'*What?*' Mr Rasi was rinsing his face in his cupped hands and he came up spluttering. 'When was this?'

'Hours ago,' said Hannah. 'I thought she'd be back by now.'

'I told her! I knew he wasn't well this morning! God protect him!'

Mr Rasi's sharp anxiety shocked Hannah.

How could I have been so callous? she thought. I've hardly thought about Susu all afternoon.

'If she'd only gone to that clinic place she'd be back by now,' Mr Rasi was saying. 'They must have sent her on to the hospital. I'd better get down there.'

He started pulling his jacket on again.

'I've made your supper, Dad,' said Hannah. 'It's all ready.'

'Supper?' Mr Rasi looked as if he'd never heard the word before. 'I couldn't . . .' He thought for a moment. 'Although, if she's gone on to the hospital I might be there till late. Yes, give me something quickly. As long as it's not too hot.'

He ate his couscous fast, standing up, then went to the door.

'You'll be all right on your own with the little

ones, Hannah?' he said as he went out. 'Don't answer the door unless it's your mother or me. If only we were in the village, where your granny and all the neighbours . . .'

'There isn't a hospital in the village,' Hannah reminded him. 'Give Susu a kiss from me.'

When he'd gone she felt like crying.

'I want Daddy,' said Karim. 'I want Mummy.'

'Yes, well, you've got me,' said Hannah. 'Come on, we'll all eat something and then I'll tell you a story.'

Mr Rasi came home very late. Hannah hadn't been able to sleep. She heard his footsteps come down the small back street and a key fumble at the lock. She got up and ran to open the door.

'What's happened? How is he?'

The lines on Mr Rasi's face looked deeper.

'It's not pneumonia. It's meningitis. They've kept him in.'

'Oh, Daddy,' said Hannah.

'Now come on,' said Mr Rasi. 'Nothing's happened yet. God willing, he'll get better. And you don't need to worry about yourself. The doctor's given me some stuff for you and the kids to stop you getting it. I'm sending off in the morning for your grandmother. Your mum'll be a lot happier when her own mother's around. Until she comes you'll stay at home and look after the children.'

'Not go to school? I can't!' Hannah saw a snapshot picture in her mind's eye of Sami waiting for her at the gate to the stork garden. 'Please, Dad. Can't we ask Mrs Rehab to look after them? She's got kids their age.'

'Your mother doesn't like her.' Mr Rasi sat down heavily and began to undo the buttons on his shirt. 'Anyway, she won't want anything to do with us when she knows there's been meningitis in the house. Now that's enough, Hannah. I'm going to bed.'

Tears welled up in Hannah's eyes. She sniffed.

'Don't cry, darling,' said Mr Rasi. 'God is merciful. Your mother's with Susu. She's looking after him. Go back to bed now.'

CHAPTER FIVE

The next three days were the longest that Hannah had ever lived through. She cooked and cleaned. She washed and fed Farida and Karim, trying to keep her temper when they cried and quarrelled, but all the time her mind was on a see-saw, up with Sami, wrapped in a golden light of happiness, or down with Susu, locked in miserable anxiety.

News had spread through the little back street and neighbours knocked on the door from time to time, offering small gifts of food or asking for news.

'Managing all on your own, are you?' Mrs Rehab said, standing well away from Hannah at the front door, her sharp eyes running round the room inside as if she was looking for a clue as to why God had struck this particular house with such a frightful disease.

'Yes, but my grandmother's coming tomorrow,' said Hannah, wanting to shut the door in her face.

'That's all right then,' Mrs Rehab said. She sounded a little disappointed.

Mr Rasi came home early on the third day. He carried a suitcase made of torn grey cardboard. Beside him hobbled an old woman dressed in black from headscarf to hem.

She climbed down the step into the house and sank gratefully on to a chair.

'My bunions!' she said. 'I don't know how I stay on my two feet. Well, goodness me, just look at Karim! Hasn't he grown? Yes, Farida, she's a lovely dolly. Clothes could do with a wash. We'll do that tomorrow. Now, Hannah, come and kiss your granny. You're a good girl. Put the kettle on, darling, and make me some tea.'

Hannah felt lighter, as if a stone had been taken off her back.

'We're out of tea, Granny,' she said. 'I couldn't get out to the shops. I couldn't leave Farida and Karim.'

'No tea?' The old woman lifted one foot on to her other knee and began to rub her aching toe joints. 'There's a shop up the road, isn't there? Just pop out and get us some.' She fished into her pocket and pulled out some coins. 'Here, take this and get yourself a few sweets while you're about it.'

The bright sunlight in the street outside was made even more dazzling by the brilliance of the white-washed walls. Hannah blinked and put up a hand to shade her eyes. She walked quickly, relishing her freedom from the children, and turned out of the alleyway into the busy shopping street.

The Golden Grocery store was on the street corner. Hannah went inside and ran her eye along the sweets displayed on the counter.

'Those ones, please,' she said, pointing to a packet of her favourite caramels, 'and two hundred and fifty grams of tea.'

The shopkeeper looked over his glasses at her as he measured out the tea leaves.

'You're Rasi's girl, aren't you?' he said. 'Sorry to hear about the baby. How's he doing?'

'Better,' said Hannah. 'The fever's down now.'

'Ah, but you never know with meningitis, do you?' the man said. 'Can leave a permanent . . .'

'Meningitis?' said a woman's voice sharply. Hannah looked round. A woman had come into the shop behind her. She was holding the end of her scarf over her mouth and looking at Hannah with widened eyes. She turned and ran out of the shop.

The shopkeeper frowned.

'No other cases down your way, are there?' he said.

Hannah shook her head.

The shopkeeper put the packet of tea down on the counter and shook his head at the coins Hannah was offering him.

'Pay me next time you're in,' he said. 'I'll make a note of it.'

'The doctor's treated us,' said Hannah, feeling angry. 'He says we can't possibly be infectious. Anyway, you'd never catch it off my money.'

'Ah, but it's better to be safe than sorry.' The

shopkeeper turned with a professional smile to the next customer who had just come into the shop. 'Yes, Madam?'

Hannah snatched up the packet of tea and the caramels and went outside.

It's like being a leper or something, she thought. Why are they all so stupid?

She was too angry to look where she was going and she stumbled over a loose paving stone. A girl who had been looking at a display of shoes in a shop window turned round, her attention attracted by the sudden movement.

'Hannah!' she squealed.

Hannah righted herself and looked up. It was Zahra.

'Hannah, where have you *been*?' Zahra grasped her arm and shook it. 'I've been frightfully worried about you. When you rushed off the other day, Muna said she'd seen you go inside the old gate. You didn't, did you? When you weren't at school I had this awful feeling you'd been murdered or kidnapped or something. That place is so spooky. I'd never dare go in on my own. I bet it's crawling with sex maniacs.'

39

Hannah managed to laugh.

'Of course I haven't been murdered,' she said. 'It's my little brother, Susu. He's been ill. He's in hospital and I've had to stay at home to look after the other two.'

'Oh, I see.' Zahra looked sideways at a reflection of herself in a shop mirror. 'What's the matter with him?'

Hannah hesitated.

'A fever,' she said. 'He's been really bad but he's better now. And my granny's come to stay so I'll be back at school on Monday.'

'Oh, good,' said Zahra. She nudged Hannah. 'That boy, you know, Sami. He's been coming to the old gate every day with Omer. He keeps asking me where you are.'

The blood rushed to Hannah's head. She shut her eyes for a brief moment as she tried to stop the ripple of shock that Sami's name had set off from showing in her face.

'What did you tell him?' She managed to sound reasonably indifferent.

'Oh, I said you'd got a rich boyfriend on the other

side of town who took you round in a gold-plated Mercedes.'

'Zahra, you *didn't*!'

Hannah stood stock still and stared at Zahra with horror.

'Only joking!' Zahra laughed. 'What are you getting so upset for, anyway? You can't like him all that much. You only met once, for five minutes.'

Her eyes were sharp with suspicion.

'Of course I don't like him,' Hannah said, looking away. 'I just don't want people to think I go round with some old guy in a car, that's all.'

Zahra seemed to lose interest in the subject.

'By the way,' she said, 'you'd better be back at school on Monday. I'm wearing my new jeans. I can't wait till everyone sees them.'

'Oh, wow!' said Hannah. 'Don't worry, I'll be there. Are you – do you reckon you'll go down to, you know, the Pepsi stall and everything, after school?'

'Yeah, probably. You want to come? You didn't stick around for long last time.'

'I don't know.' Hannah tried to sound unconcerned. 'It depends on how Susu is. I'll see.'

'Hope he's better soon,' said Zahra, veering off down the side road that led to her house. 'See you on Monday!'

CHAPTER SIX

'I need you, Hannah,' said Granny the next morning. 'There's something I want you to do.'

Hannah's mouth turned down at the corners. She had a plan for the weekend. She was going to do something new with her hair and mend her prettiest blouse. After that she was going to find somewhere very quiet and peaceful, perhaps on the roof of the house, and there she was going to write a poem about Sami.

'Don't look sour, miss,' said Granny. 'Someone's got to do it. I'd go myself, but I can't walk that far.'

'What is it?' said Hannah, knowing she'd have to

give in. There was never any point in arguing with Granny.

The old woman hitched her dress up and squatted down beside the plateful of lentils she was picking over.

'I'm not happy about Susu,' she said. 'If the fever's gone down, why aren't they letting him out of hospital? I don't like the sound of it.'

Hannah looked down, puzzled, at the top of her grandmother's head.

'I can't do anything about Susu, Gran,' she said.

'Yes you can,' Granny said positively. She straightened her shoulders, bridling a little. 'Just because I've lived in the village all my life it doesn't mean this is the first time I've come to town. Last time I came was with your auntie. Must have been ten years ago. We went to the holy man's tomb down by the river – Sidi Ben Daoud. You take the bus to the bottom of the hill, then there's a path . . .'

'I know where it is, Gran,' said Hannah.

'She was in such agony, she could hardly stand up. A week later it had gone! She was completely cured! So I want you to go down there, Hannah,

44

and find the little opening at the side of the tomb and say a prayer into it.'

'What prayer?' Hannah was half irritated, half amused.

'You can pray for your brother however you like,' said Granny with dignity. 'But recite a piece from the Holy Koran as well, and if you can't do that, then heaven knows what all this going to school is good for!'

'Granny . . .' began Hannah.

Her grandmother stood up and put a hand on Hannah's shoulder. She was shorter than Hannah but strength flowed out of her.

'There's mysteries about health and sickness,' she said, 'and only an ignorant fool thinks fancy western doctors know everything. Superstition's one thing, but spiritual power's something else. You get along to that holy man's tomb and pray for Susu. You're not going to tell me you refuse?'

'It's not that, Granny.' Hannah frowned. 'It's just that the girls at school say it's a really bad place down by the river. All the drug dealers go there.'

'Nonsense.' Granny squatted down and began to

work over the lentils again. 'I went there with your grandad before you were born. And then I took your auntie there ten years ago. It was lovely. Really quiet. No one about but a few holy pilgrims. They'd never hurt a young girl.'

'But that was ten years ago! There weren't any drug dealers around then.'

'Don't think I'm stupid, Hannah. There've always been criminals around. No more excuses, now. Don't you love your brother?'

'Please, Gran. Can't I wait till Dad gets home and go with him?'

'Men!' The old woman shook her head vigorously. 'They've got no real religion, any of them! Your father wouldn't dream of going to Sidi Ben Daoud. He'd call it idle superstition. It's a woman's job, Hannah, and you've got to do it. Get going and you'll be back in time for lunch.'

CHAPTER SEVEN

A busy road ran down the hill towards the river. Hannah knew it well. She'd ridden along it in the bus on her way to school every day since she'd come to the city. But she'd never walked along the cracked and broken pavement before, and she felt conspicuous. Buses and trucks roared past, choking black diesel fumes belching out of their exhausts. She was afraid that the people inside them might be looking at her.

At the bottom of the hill the main road curved round to the left, and a wooded lane, too narrow for cars, led off to the right along the bank of the river. The tomb was about half a kilometre further on. Hannah had often seen it from the bus. It was a simple, square building of whitewashed stone with a dome on top, built on a small platform of stone that jutted out into the river.

The lane was cool and shaded. Trees in their bright spring foliage hung over it and the river sucked and gurgled in the reeds at the water's edge. Hannah hesitated before she started down it. The lane was empty as far ahead as she could see, but its very quietness was sinister.

I suppose it's all right, she said to herself. I can't see anyone, anyway.

She took a few hesitant steps along the muddy path.

Susu, she thought. I've just got to keep thinking about Susu.

She pulled her scarf closely round her face and began to walk faster, skirting the puddles, alert to every small sound. After a few minutes she rounded the first bend. Now the main road was no longer in sight and even the traffic was only a distant roar. Her contact with the everyday world of the streets and people of the city had been broken. She was on her own.

There was a rustle in the long grass beside her and she jumped with fright, her skin prickling all over. She'd never been in such a place before. She'd never felt so alone.

The rustling stopped. The lizard or the snake which had caused it had slipped away, but the thumping of Hannah's heart hadn't stopped. She could hear it pounding in her ears.

It can't be far now, she thought. I must've walked miles already.

Another bend was just ahead. She could hear voices beyond it. Were they coming towards her, or moving away? She stood still, poised to turn and run. But it was too late for that. If they were coming her way she would never get out of sight before she was seen. She looked from side to side, her mind racing. The trees that fringed the lane were densely packed. She wouldn't be able to force her way into the thorny undergrowth that grew beneath them.

If the worst comes to the worst I'll jump into the river, she thought wildly. I only think I can't swim. I'm sure I could if I really had to.

She realized that the voices had grown fainter.

Whoever it was must have been walking away from her after all. She walked on quickly, grateful that the quiet swishing of the water against the bank muffled the sound of her feet.

The path was strewn with litter. Old pieces of paper were wrapped round the tree roots and rusting cans and pieces of broken glass lay tossed among the stones.

A shout close behind made her freeze again. She couldn't think rationally this time. She couldn't measure the distance to the next bend in the lane or work out her chances of drowning if she jumped into the river. The shout came again. It was a man's voice, high-pitched and angry. Hannah broke into a run. She had to find a place to hide! She had to squeeze herself into the cleft of a tree, or throw herself into a clump of reeds, or –

She raced round the next corner and saw, straight ahead, a small white building. She'd reached the tomb. It stood squarely on its little stone outcrop, gleaming white in the morning sun, and the water lapped against its foundations on the side that faced the river.

Hannah gasped with relief and ran round it to hide on the far side. She could hear the man shouting again. He was coming up fast towards the tomb. When he passed it, she'd be in full view. She had to get round behind to the side that faced the river. She'd have to get into the water.

Gingerly she put her foot down through the rushes, feeling for the bottom. The water ran at once into her shoe, but she had no time to worry about that. She stepped further in, afraid of falling into the depths and being carried away downstream, but even more afraid of the man with the demented voice who was coming closer and closer.

'Hosni! You lousy creep! I know you're here! Come on out or I'll kill you!'

The plaster of the tomb's wall was rough under Hannah's hand as she leaned against it, feeling the way with her feet. The water was no more than knee deep. She was quite out of sight from the lane now. Only someone coming right to the river's edge and leaning out over the water would be able to see her.

The man had come level with the tomb. He was standing where she'd been a few seconds earlier.

Hannah could hear his feet crunching on the loose stones. He was no more than three or four metres away from her. She felt half paralysed with terror, her knees weak, her hands shaking as she clung to the old stone wall.

'Hosni!' The man's tone had changed to a whine. 'Don't torture me! I'll pay whatever you asked! You promised!'

His words disintegrated into an irregular muttering. Hannah could hear his footsteps again. He was moving away, talking to himself, stumbling along the path, going further along the lane.

Hannah found that she couldn't move. The danger had passed, she was alone again, but she couldn't bear to come out from behind the shelter of the tomb. Then, from a little way upstream, she heard a rhythmic splashing. A boat was being rowed towards her round the bend of the river. The sound was somehow reassuring. Fishermen went out in boats. They wouldn't be likely to stop and bother someone beside a holy tomb.

The sound came closer. She could see the prow already, coming round the corner.

They'll think I'm mad, she thought, just standing here up to my knees in water.

Embarrassment gave her the courage to splash back out of the river to the narrow ledge at the side of the tomb. She looked up and down the lane. No one was coming from either direction.

I'll run fast all the way back to the road, she told herself. It's not that far.

Her feet were squelching in her sodden shoes. She took them off and shook the water out of them. As she bent down to put them on again she saw something small and pink lying by the wall of the tomb. It was a baby bird that must have fallen from its nest. It was dead from hunger or exposure.

Susu! thought Hannah. I nearly forgot him!

She hurried round to the front of the tomb. A small hole, no bigger than an arrow slit, made a dark gash in the bright white wall. Someone had laid flowers on the ground beneath it and the hole itself was worn where thousands of hands had touched it.

Hannah put her own hand into the hole. The stone inside felt cool against her fingers and a slight draught blew on them. Though she was frightened and longed to run away, a little of the stillness from inside the dark interior crept over her and made her feel stronger.

In the name of God, the Compassionate, the Merciful, she murmured. Remember Susu. Help Susu.

She hadn't been sure that she would know what to say but as she stood there words from the Koran came tumbling from her lips.

> He brings forth the living from the dead.
> And the dead from the living.
> The lifeless earth is quickened by Him.
> Likewise shall you be raised to life.

She closed her eyes for a moment and saw Susu. He was asleep in his crib, his red lips slightly parted, his eyelids twitching a little as he dreamed.

He can't be harmed, she thought. He's just a little baby. He's got to get better.

The rowing boat was nearly alongside the tomb now and the two men in it had seen her. One of them called out, 'Hello, love! God will answer your prayers, don't worry!'

The other waved too.

'Good luck!' he shouted.

Hannah waved back at them. Here, at the saint's tomb, where the light shone clear on the white walls and glittered on the wavelets of the river, everything seemed normal. She felt protected. But the entrance to the lane that would take her back to the real world was a dark mouth, the overhanging trees plunging it in shadow. She would have to leave this holy place and enter it again.

She touched the hole in the wall once more and bent down to kiss the sill.

God protect me, she whispered. Keep me safe.

A bird on a tree by the entrance to the lane began to sing.

If it flies off and lands on the tomb I'll be safe, she thought. If it flies over the river I'll be in danger.

The bird stayed still. She watched it for a moment.

I'm just being superstitious, she thought. I'm as bad as Granny.

She waited for a moment longer but the bird didn't move.

A cloud suddenly covered the sun. She looked

up. It was as dark as indigo and heavy with rain. With the sunshine gone she no longer felt so safe, but there was no point in clinging to the tomb any longer. She had to brave the return journey.

She began to walk quickly back down the lane.

It's not so far, she kept telling herself. I've gone ten metres already. I've gone twenty metres. Thirty. Forty . . .

Raindrops pattered on the leaves overhead. They comforted her. Fewer people were likely to come down here during a storm. She'd be safer in the rain. She began to walk fast, clutching her headscarf close round her face.

She didn't see the man until she was almost alongside him. He'd been standing still at the side of the path in a gap in the wall of trees, watching her approach.

'Hey, hey!' he said, almost in her ear. 'She's pretty! What's she doing here, all alone?'

Hannah leaped back in terror. The man stumbled towards her. He was unshaven and his clothes were dirty. His hair was long and matted and his eyes were hazy.

'Come here,' he said thickly. 'If you know what's good for you, you'll do what you're told.'

'Go away,' said Hannah, backing away from him. She knew her voice was trembling but she couldn't speak more firmly. 'Don't touch me!'

The man laughed.

'Why not? 'S just what I fancy. If you don't want it, what d'you come down here for, all on your own?'

Hannah tried to run but her shoes, still heavy with river water, weighed her down and before she'd taken more than a couple of steps the man's long hand shot out and he was gripping her wrist painfully.

'Let's see what you're like, my little pigeon, my little plump pigeon,' he muttered. 'Tasty little . . .'

'No!' screamed Hannah, pushing away the fingers that were fumbling at the front of her dress. Her head was reeling with nausea at the disgusting smell of alcohol and stale sweat that rolled off his body.

She felt his hold on her arm momentarily slacken and with a sudden violent movement she wrenched herself away, pushed past him and began to run, faster than she'd ever run before. She heard him curse and his feet splash through the puddles as he ran after her but she didn't dare turn round in case she fell.

She thought he was just behind her, she could see in her mind's eye his reddened face leering and his hand reaching out to clutch at her shoulder, but at the very moment when she was sure he was about to catch her again she burst out of the lane into the main road.

She looked back. The man was some way behind but he was still coming after her, and even though he was swaying in a strange way and his arms and legs seemed out of control he looked strong and fast.

The hill was ahead of her now, the broken pavement rising up alongside the busy roadway. She didn't care if the people in the buses and trucks stared at her. She didn't notice the rain, drenching her hair and soaking her clothes. She just wanted to escape as fast as she could, to run home, shut the door behind her, bolt it, wash herself, change all her clothes and creep under her bed to hide.

Her heart was pounding. Her chest rasped pain-fully as she gasped for breath. She didn't dare look round again.

A bicycle, coming down the hill towards her, suddenly skidded to a halt as the boy riding it caught sight of her. He jumped off.

'Hannah!' he shouted.

She looked round. It was Sami.

Chapter Eight

'Sami!' Hannah looked fearfully behind her. The drunk man had stopped running. He was turning back, staggering off down the hill. 'Oh thank God! I'm safe!'

Sami hadn't noticed him. He was scowling at the traffic going up and down the road. Already another bicycle had stopped close by and a man riding down the road on a donkey was twisting round to watch them.

'What are you *doing* here?' said Sami. 'Everyone's looking at you! What's been going on?'

He sounded angry. Hannah was panting for breath but her pants turned to sobs. Now he despises me. He despises me! was all she could think.

He put a hand under her elbow and, steering his bike with the other, led her away from the edge of the road. A little way further up the hill a broken-down wall gave on to a yard surrounded by derelict farm buildings which had long since been swallowed up by the growing city. Sami pushed Hannah through the opening and hauled his bicycle in after them.

They were in a small courtyard, surrounded on all sides by broken-down walls. People had been here before them and had used one corner as a toilet, but the other end was clean. Sami led Hannah across to a pile of large fallen stones sheltered by the remains of an old roof. She sank down on to them, dropped her face into her hands and burst into tears.

'*Tell* me!' Sami said. 'Has someone hurt you? Just tell me who it was and I'll go and kill him!'

Hannah shuddered.

'I don't know. A horrible drunk man. Down there.'

She waved her hand in the direction of the river.

'What did he *do*? Did he touch you? If he did I'll . . .'

'He didn't really,' Hannah was frightened by the

61

fierceness in his voice. 'I was just scared. There was no one else there. It was . . .'

'I can't understand any of this.' Sami, ignoring the rain, marched up and down the tiny courtyard, kicking out at the small stones that littered it. 'What on earth were you doing down by the river, anyway? I mean, you must have known . . .'

'It was Granny!' burst out Hannah. 'She made me . . .'

'Your *grandmother*?' Sami stopped kicking at the stones and looked at her incredulously. '*She* sent you right into . . .'

'Yes, but she didn't realize!' Hannah wanted so desperately to make the frown disappear from his face that the words were almost choking her. 'I had to go to the tomb. To be near Sidi Ben Daoud. To pray! Susu's got – he's in hospital!'

'Who the hell's Susu?' said Sami, and his brows snapped jealously together.

'My little brother. He's only a baby. He's been desperately ill. That's why I haven't been . . .'

'That's why you haven't been coming to the stork garden? Oh, Hannah!' Sami had been walking stiffly, rigid with anger, but he suddenly relaxed. He came back to the pile of stones and sat down beside her. 'I thought you'd only been pretending that time. I thought maybe you were just a tease, like Zahra. I've been going out of my mind! I waited at the gate every day, desperately hoping you'd come. You can't imagine how miserable I've been.'

'Oh, I do know! It's been awful!' Hannah had stopped crying. She sniffed and wiped her eyes on the end of her scarf. 'I couldn't get a message to you or anything. I thought Zahra would at least tell you I hadn't been coming to school.'

'Zahra! She wouldn't tell me anything! All she did was go on and on with her stupid teasing, about how you'd got some rich boyfriend with a Merc and that you'd . . .'

'She didn't!' Hannah sat up, red spots of indignation in her cheeks. 'That's it! I'll never speak to her again!'

Sami took her hand. He began to play with her fingers.

'Then I didn't imagine it?' he said. 'You do love me?'

His hand was hot and trembling. He was sitting very close to her now. She edged away.

'Yes! Yes, of course I . . .'

He put his arm round her and pulled her towards him. She felt his warmth through his thin wet shirt and it dazed and confused her. She couldn't believe that such a thing was happening. She didn't know what to do. He pulled her closer. The stones dug uncomfortably into her thigh and she tried to move away. He was breathing heavily. He bent his head, trying to find her lips. She caught a faint whiff of his sweat and it mingled with the bad smells in the courtyard. All of a sudden, the foul stink of the drunk man was in her nostrils. It was his hands that were touching her blouse.

She scrambled to her feet.

'Please, Sami! Don't!'

He stood up, too, and pulled her roughly into his arms.

'Don't play games with me,' he said hoarsely. 'Don't be like the others. I love you. I'll never do anything to hurt you.'

He was trying to kiss her again, forcing her head up.

'Stop it!' she whispered. 'Leave me alone!'

She pushed him away with all her strength and ran to the gap in the wall.

'Hannah, don't go!' said Sami. 'Wait!'

But she was through the wall and out in the road already, running up the hill.

'Come back!' she heard him shout after her. 'I didn't mean . . . Meet me tomorrow afternoon, in the stork garden. Please, Hannah! Please!'

CHAPTER NINE

Hannah ran almost all the way home. The rain had stopped while she'd been with Sami and her clothes had almost dried by the time she reached the alleyway. Her mother opened the door. Hannah threw her arms round her.

'Oh Mum! Mum!' she panted. She wanted to tell her everything that had happened but she didn't dare. Instead she said, 'Where's Susu? Is he all right? I didn't know you were coming back today!'

'Watch out. You'll break my ribs.' Mrs Rasi detached herself. 'What's the matter with you? Where have you been? What's all the hurry?'

Over her mother's shoulder, Hannah saw Granny

silently move her lips. She looked pale and nervous. She'd always been a little afraid of her sharp-tongued daughter.

'Don't say anything,' she mouthed. Hannah had never seen such a pleading look in an adult's face. She gave Granny a tiny nod.

'Zahra came to see me,' she said to her mother. 'We've been round the shops.'

'Why bother?' Mrs Rasi took down a bag of onions and began to peel one. 'You can't afford to buy anything. There'll be nothing to spend in this house for a long time, not until we've paid for all these expensive medicines.'

She began to chop the onions. Granny caught Hannah's eye and lifted her eyebrows in a question. Hannah nodded again. A smile broke out over the old lady's face, spreading a network of deep wrinkles through her brown, leathery skin.

Mrs Rasi looked up.

'Aren't you going to ask me how your brother is?' she said.

'I did,' said Hannah. 'How is he? Have you brought him home? Is he here?'

'Of course I've brought him home! You don't think I'd leave him with a whole parcel of strangers? He's over there, asleep, poor little soul.'

She nodded towards the crib in the corner of the room. Hannah went over to look. Susu lay on his back, asleep. He looked thin and pale. One small hand was above the blanket, which he was clutching even in his sleep.

'He looks smaller,' said Hannah doubtfully.

'He is. He's lost more than a kilo.'

Hannah felt a stab of anxiety.

'He'll be all right though, Mum, won't he?'

Mrs Rasi pursed her lips. There were rings of tiredness round her eyes and her mouth had settled into a thin line of anxiety.

'Wait and see, that's all they'd say. He's out of danger, but it's whether he'll be all right in the head. "Give him a day to sleep the fever off," the doctor said. "If he's not himself again in a day or two you'll have grounds to worry."'

'There's no need to worry at all,' Granny said comfortingly, patting Hannah's forearm with her calloused hand. 'Susu's going to be right as rain. You mark my words.'

'You sound very certain,' Mrs Rasi said drily.

Granny smiled.

'Oh, I am,' she said. 'I am.'

Hannah went into the next room.

'Where are you going?' Mrs Rasi called out. 'Don't slip off! I'm going to need you in a minute.'

'I only want to wash,' Hannah called back. 'I feel all hot and dirty.'

She went to the bathroom and shut the door. Her legs were shaky. She wanted to scrub herself from head to toe, to wash away everything that had happened. She couldn't bear to think about the man in the lane, his reeking breath, his clutching hands. She didn't want to think about Sami, either. She wasn't ready. Not yet.

'Hannah!'

Someone was tapping softly at the bathroom door. Hannah opened it a crack. Granny stood there.

'Hannah, I'm so sorry,' she whispered. 'I should have listened to you. I said something about the

69

tomb to your mother. What you said was right. It really is a bad place now. I've been so worried about you. It was too late to do anything, so I was going to wait till your father got home and send him down to look for you.'

'It's all right, Granny,' said Hannah.

'Did you have any trouble? Did anyone bother you?'

Granny's blue-filmed eyes were bright with concern.

'No,' said Hannah. 'No bother. Nothing really happened. I got to the tomb and said a prayer for Susu and a piece from the Koran like you told me to.'

'You're a good girl.' Granny shifted her bulk comfortably from one foot to the other. 'Your prayer will be answered. You'll see. Susu's going to be himself again.'

She went away. Hannah closed the bathroom door.

'Why did you do it, Sami?' she whispered. 'Why did you have to go and spoil everything?'

CHAPTER TEN

Hannah slept badly that night. She tossed around, trying to find a comfortable position, but every time she was about to drop off to sleep, she sensed that the man in the lane was standing at the door, or peering in at her through the window, and she started up awake.

Was it me? she thought. Was it my fault? Perhaps if I'd prayed harder, or run faster . . .

She turned over again.

Why can't I just forget him? He was a horrible old drunk, that's all. It was nothing to do with me.

She forced herself not to think about him. Instead,

Sami's face, flushed as he tried to kiss her, swam into her mind.

He's not really like that, she thought. He's not a bullying type of person. He's kind and good. It's like Mum says, men get carried away sometimes. And there we were, not expecting to see each other, and I was all upset and he was angry . . .

She shifted her shoulders, trying to find a softer place. Granny, sleeping beside her, rolled over on to her back and began to snore.

Should I go to the stork garden tomorrow? Hannah thought, staring with wide-open eyes at the crack in the shutters, through which a chink of moonlight shone into the room. What if he's rough and angry again? I won't go. I couldn't bear it.

She sighed, and into her nostrils came a faint whiff of the rose-scented powder which Granny used to dust her feet. At once she remembered the carpet of wild flowers in the garden through which she and Sami had wandered hand in hand, and she was flooded once more with the same wonderful feeling of happiness, as if her soul was flying like the stork on up-tilted wings. Her eyelids felt heavy at last and the bed was suddenly comfortable. She gave a mighty yawn and fell asleep.

Just before dawn, the early morning call to prayer echoed in haunting beauty across the quiet city, from the minaret by the central mosque. Hannah stirred in her sleep, but didn't wake.

Noisy chatterings from the next room roused her early. Susu was awake. Hannah pulled the covers over her ears, trying in vain to block out the sound and go back to sleep. Then she heard her mother laughing happily and she remembered everything and sat up.

She ran into the next room. Susu was sitting on his parents' bed, hiding his face under a corner of the sheet.

'Where's Susu?' Mr Rasi was saying, tickling his baby son's foot.

Susu pulled the sheet off his face and bounced up and down, crowing with laughter.

'*There* he is!' said Mrs Rasi, snatching him up in her arms.

Hannah saw that she was crying.

73

'What's the matter, Mum?' she said. 'Is he still ill?'

'No!' said Mrs Rasi. 'He's better! He's himself again! Look at him, smiling, laughing . . .'

Mr Rasi took Susu out of his wife's arms so that she could wipe her eyes and blow her nose, but she couldn't stop crying and rocked herself backwards and forwards, tears glistening on her cheeks.

'Don't, Mum,' said Hannah, putting her arms round her. 'It's all right.'

Mrs Rasi hugged her back.

'Yes, thank God! I didn't dare ask the doctor much, and he only said we'd know more or less at once if he was going to be all right, but the nurse kept telling me about her husband's niece, how she'd had meningitis and gone deaf . . .'

She started crying again.

'What's going on?' Granny stood in the doorway, clutching the opening of her nightdress together with one mottled hand.

'Susu's better!' said Hannah. 'He's fine!'

Mr Rasi, afraid that his mother-in-law would start crying too, heaved Susu up on to his shoulder and groped for his slippers with his feet.

74

'I'll take him into the other room,' he said hastily, and went out.

Granny came in and sat down on the bed.

'I told you!' she said triumphantly. 'Well done, Hannah!'

Mrs Rasi wiped her eyes.

'I don't know what it's got to do with Hannah,' she said. 'Though you've been a very good girl.' She looked down at her hands and twisted her old silver ring round her finger. 'I've been a bit hasty with you lately, I know,' she said. 'Don't mind me. It's just all the worry of moving and getting used to living here and Susu . . .'

Hannah felt tears prick her own eyes. The world had been shaken about but she could feel something solid under her feet again.

'It's OK, Mum,' she said. 'I sort of knew it wasn't anything to do with me.' She made a decision and took a deep breath. 'I've got to tell her, Gran. It's not right, keeping it a secret.'

Granny shook her head and her mouth formed a silent no.

'Tell me what?' The sharpness, which had all but

gone from Mrs Rasi's voice, threatened to return.

'I went to Sidi Ben Daoud's tomb yesterday, on my own, to pray for Susu,' said Hannah, not daring to look at her mother.

'I didn't know it was dangerous!' Granny's voice rose in a wail. 'You've got to believe me, when I went there with your auntie, there were only pilgrims, holy people! I had no idea it was a haunt of criminals and drug dealers!'

'Did anything happen to you?' Mrs Rasi turned her back on her mother and shook Hannah's arm. 'Did anyone touch you?'

'No, Mum, it's OK,' said Hannah. 'There was a horrible man, he was drunk and he tried to . . . he tried to grab me, but I ran away.'

'He didn't hurt you? Are you sure?' Mrs Rasi was searching Hannah's face. 'He didn't do anything to you?'

'No! He stank. Oh, it was horrible!' Talking about it felt good. Hannah wanted to tell them everything, to describe every small detail. 'His hair was all long and dirty and he was staggering. He grabbed my arm and said he wanted to – to do things to me.'

'Yes?' Mrs Rasi's voice was shrill.

'I shook him off and ran away. I was shaking all over. I've never been so scared in my whole life.'

'Did he follow you?'

'Yes, but not far.' Hannah saw in her mind's eye Sami squealing to a halt on his bicycle and shut out the thought of him. 'I ran all the way home.'

'Oh, my darling,' Mrs Rasi hugged her again. 'If anything had happened to you . . .'

'God protected her,' said Granny, nodding her head. 'She was on a holy pilgrimage and . . .'

'Yes, well,' Mrs Rasi's face was stony. 'But you should never have sent her off on such a . . .'

'Susu wants his bottle!' Mr Rasi called out from the next room. 'He's hungry.'

'And Susu is better,' said Granny, watching her daughter's face nervously. 'God answered Hannah's prayers. You can't deny that.'

Susu toddled into the room on unsteady feet, his nappy trailing. Mrs Rasi's face softened.

'So he did,' she said, scooping the baby up. 'So he did.' She smiled at Hannah. 'After all, there's no need to tell your father,' she whispered.

CHAPTER ELEVEN

B reakfast was a hilarious meal that Sunday morning. Even Karim and Farida, who had slept until late, were infected with excitement. They dashed about, chasing each other round the table at which their elders were sitting, until Karim tripped over and bumped his knee.

'Now come on, there's no need to scream like that,' said Mr Rasi, giving the little boy a cuddle. 'Look at Farida. She fell over but she didn't make a fuss.' He stood up. 'I'm going out,' he said. 'I'll stop by at the hospital and leave a message for the doctor. He said to let him know how Susu was this morning.'

'Mum,' said Hannah quickly, before she lost her

courage. 'Can I go out this afternoon? Zahra and some of the girls from school are going to the old city.'

Mr Rasi had reached the door, but he turned back.

'The old city?' he said. 'Where all the storks' nests are?'

He looked at his wife and the corners of his eyes creased as he smiled. Mrs Rasi was smiling back at him, shaking her head as if she was ashamed by her own softness. They seemed to be sharing a delightful secret.

They didn't meet there like us when they were young! They couldn't have! thought Hannah, shocked. She gave her head a tiny shake. Of course they didn't! They were living in the village!

'Well, I don't know . . .' Mrs Rasi was saying.

'A group of you? All going together?' said Mr Rasi. 'Why not? Tell you what, if I come back in time, I might take you all down there myself. You could get a picnic ready. We haven't been in that old place for ages. What do you say?'

Hannah held her breath but Mrs Rasi shook her head.

'What are you thinking of?' she said. 'I can't take Susu out yet. He's only just out of hospital. And I've got a terrible pile of washing to catch up with.'

Mr Rasi nodded and went out. Hannah let her breath go slowly.

'I'll help you with the washing before I go out, Mum,' she said, hating herself for being deceitful.

'No, no,' Mrs Rasi stood up and started gathering the dishes together. 'You deserve a rest after all you've been through.'

Perhaps I won't go to the stork garden after all, thought Hannah. It must be wrong, if it makes me feel so guilty. But then she thought, I'll go, but only so I can tell Sami I won't see him again.

She stood up and caught sight of herself in the mirror above the basin. She thought she looked ugly and childish. She tried scraping her hair back away from her face, but it wouldn't fall in the way she wanted.

I can't see Sami looking like this! she thought. And what on earth am I going to wear?

By early afternoon, Hannah was feeling sick with nerves. She stood at the mirror, brushing her hair, trying unsuccessfully to make the ends turn up like Zahra's did.

Supposing Dad found out I was secretly meeting a boy, she thought. He'd go mad. He really, really would.

Granny appeared behind her.

'Here, let me do that,' she said, taking the brush out of Hannah's hands. 'Oh my, what lovely hair! It's so silky and soft. Reminds me of my mother. She had hair like yours.'

She began to plait it.

'Please, Gran,' said Hannah. 'I want to leave it loose. That's what all the other girls do.'

'Loose?'

Granny looked shocked.

'I'll put my scarf over it. You won't see it, really you won't. It's just that it feels more comfortable.'

Mrs Rasi came into the room.

'Are you wearing your blue skirt, love? Do you want me to iron it for you?'

'Yes – no! The red one! Don't bother about it, Mum, please!'

She wanted to shout 'Leave me alone, can't you?'

but she didn't want to hurt their feelings. She finished dressing as quickly as she could, dragged the scarf over her hair and slipped on her shoes.

'Goodbye, dear,' said Granny. 'Have a nice time. Be careful, now.'

'Mind you're not late home,' said Mrs Rasi.

Hannah rushed to the door.

'Wait a minute,' Granny said. 'Look, here's a little something so you can buy yourself a Pepsi.' She began to fumble in one pocket after another, looking for a coin.

'It's all right, Gran,' said Hannah. 'I don't need any money.' And she ran out of the door. She pulled it shut by the old brass knocker. She wanted to bang it violently but she didn't.

She stood outside for a moment. She needed time to shake off her irritation before she screwed up her courage to go. Her mother's voice came clearly through the open window.

'It's not been easy for Hannah. It's so different here. The kids are stuck up and much too indepen-dent and what their mothers are thinking of I'm sure I don't know, letting them . . .'

Hannah defiantly took off her scarf and let her hair hang long and free, then she began to hurry down the street towards the bus stop.

The bus was half empty. Hannah sat near the back, pleating her fingers in and out of the folds of her skirt.

I'm mad. This is crazy. I'm a bad girl, she thought. I never dreamed I'd do anything like this. I'll get off at the next stop and go home.

But she stayed on the bus. It pulled up at last at her usual stop for school and she got off and began to walk down towards the Paradise Gate. In the distance the clock on the tower of the National Bank began to strike. One ... Hannah waited for the second chime. It didn't come.

Only one o'clock! She thought. I'm much too early. He didn't say a time, only the afternoon, but he won't be here for ages. What am I going to do? I can't just hang around. I'll be seen. I'll get bothered by men.

She nearly turned back towards the town. It would be safer walking down the main street where there would be plenty of other people. No one would be likely to notice her there.

But I'd bump into Zahra, I bet I would, she thought. She'll be going to the cinema. She always does on a Sunday afternoon. I'd never get away from her if she saw me and she might guess something.

She went on more slowly towards the gate.

I'll go into the stork garden and hide somewhere. No one goes there. I'll find a place and just stay there quietly and look out for him.

The decision made her stronger. She reached the gate and slipped through it.

In the shade of the wall, an old man was dozing on a fallen marble pillar. His head lolled back and the white stubble on his chin pointed to the sky. He heard her light footfall, woke up and looked at her. For a moment Hannah thought he was going to beg for money, or tell her she wasn't allowed in, but he only smiled and mumbled something. It sounded like, 'May God give you your heart's desire.'

He couldn't have said that, said Hannah to herself as she picked her way down the path, choosing the bare stones to walk on so that her feet wouldn't make a noise on the loose gravel. He couldn't know why I'm here. He'd shout at me and call me names if he did.

She reached the paved area where she'd stood with Sami on that blissful afternoon and hesitated. She wanted to wait here, but it was too open. Anyone coming down the path would see her. She went on down the hill, looking out for a good place to hide.

The storks were quiet this afternoon. She could see three nests now and each one had a solitary bird on it. They sat quietly on their eggs, their long wings folded, their beaks resting on their feathered chests, waiting for their mates to return and relieve them. Hannah was grateful for their stillness. Like her, they didn't want to be noticed.

The path had been going down in a series of shallow steps for some time and it turned sharply at the bottom, where it came out of the trees. Hannah stepped into the open and looked round cautiously, but she couldn't see anyone and nothing moved, except for a pair of pigeons which were strutting and cooing on the old worn flagstones.

She had arrived at the ruins. To one side were the broken walls of what might once have been a palace or a mosque. On the other, some fig trees had seeded themselves long ago and had forced their way up through the old stone floor, which was buckled by their roots.

Straight ahead, in the shadow of the fig trees, was a square hole in the ground. Hannah crept forward to look, and stared down into a pool of water. Steps descended into it and she could see, through arches on one side, where the water went on into a cavernous recess underground.

The pool was shaded and still. Then a withered leaf which was lying on the surface began to rock a little and under it Hannah saw something long and supple and dark, winding its way through the water.

A snake! she thought, starting back, but then she remembered the pool in the river below the village at home.

Not a snake. Only an eel.

She relaxed again.

She could see another now, and another. They came slipping out of the darkness through the arches, their long grey bodies moving so sinuously they hardly stirred the water.

They're not really frightening at all, thought Hannah. Only beautiful and strange.

'Have you got the eggs?'

A voice not far behind her made her jump. A woman was speaking, old by the sound of her, and still just out of sight, and footsteps were coming closer and closer down the steps towards the pool.

'Yes, Auntie,' a younger woman said impatiently. 'You've asked me three times already.'

Hannah slipped away from the pool, through a broken archway into the old ruins near by. The roof had long since fallen in and in some places the walls had crumbled almost to nothing. It would be easy to get out, to find another way up the hill from here towards the old gateway. She could avoid the main path altogether.

The clock in the distance struck two. Hannah's heart thumped.

He might be here already, she thought. He might have come early, like me.

She scrambled over a low wall and out of the ruins. She could see a narrow path now, a little overgrown but quite passable, winding through the trees up the hill. She began to climb it. The two women had reached the pool and Hannah could hear their voices easily.

'Oh Auntie,' the younger one was saying, and her voice was breaking with tears. 'What if it doesn't work? I can't bear another disappointment! I don't think I could go on living!'

The older woman's voice was soothing.

'Don't give up hope, my darling. God is great. Feed the eels. Look, here they come.'

CHAPTER TWELVE

Hannah came out on to the main path near the top of the hill and saw Sami bounding down towards her. He caught hold of her hands and they stood for a long moment looking at each other. Her heart moved strangely in her chest.

'You came! I didn't think you would!' he said, and his face was flushed with joy.

Voices came from above. Other people were on their way down to the pool.

'I know a place where we can talk,' said Sami.

He led Hannah off the main path. She looked over her shoulder, afraid of being seen.

I've got to tell him I won't meet him again, she

said to herself, but she followed him, ducking under the low branches he held out of her way.

They came out into a clearing. A building had stood here long ago. All that remained of it was a square of paving and some tumbled stones, warm in the sun.

Sami sat down on an old wall and Hannah, who had been afraid he would try to kiss her again, sat down timidly beside him.

'I felt so awful on Saturday!' Sami burst out. 'You'd had a terrible experience and you'd been frightened and I should have listened to you! I should have run after whoever it was and beaten him up!'

'Oh no,' said Hannah. 'It wouldn't have been worth it.'

Her confidence was growing and with it came joy. She didn't want anything to spoil it. She didn't want to remember the man in the lane.

Sami was looking at her, his expression earnest, intent.

'I feel I've lost the right to say I love you,' he said.

'You haven't,' said Hannah, in a small voice.

Her eyes were fixed on his hands which were gripping the stones of the wall he was sitting on. His fingers were long and slim and his forearms brown and muscular.

'I know girls need more time,' Sami was saying. 'I was so full of – of the way I felt, and I just didn't think!' He hit his forehead with the palm of his hand. 'There! I've done it again!' He began to pummel his knees with bunched fists. 'I meant to ask you as soon as I saw you about your brother. I couldn't believe you did that, risked going to such a scary place, to pray for him. I mean, it was so brave!'

'Susu's fine,' said Hannah. 'He really is. He was already home from the hospital when I got back and this morning he was fine! I mean laughing and playing like he usually does. The doctor said . . .'

'It's just so great the way you love him like that,' said Sami. 'You feel things really deeply. You're the kind of person who . . .'

Hannah was looking down at his hand again. It was moving slowly towards hers. She felt the tingle in her fingers before he touched her. He shifted along the wall a little way towards her. She knew she ought to stand up and tell him she couldn't see him again but she couldn't move. His head was bending towards hers now and her eyes were fixed on his lips. She smelled the warm freshness of his breath for a moment and then his mouth touched hers. The incredible sweetness of his touch lit up her whole being before she pulled away from him.

It's no good. We mustn't, she wanted to say, but he spoke first.

'Don't be frightened. I'm not going to hurt you. I'll never be rough with you again.'

His arm was round her now. She allowed herself to rest within its circle and never before had she felt so safe.

They sat in silence for what seemed like a long time looking into each others' eyes. They didn't need to speak. The whole universe had shrunk to this small clearing in the trees. The entire world was enclosed in the space between them.

'This is our special place,' Sami said at last. 'We'll be safe here. We can come whenever we like and be here alone.'

'No,' whispered Hannah, shaking her head. 'I can't! We mustn't!'

But Sami didn't seem to hear. He was looking away from her, into the trees.

'We've got the whole summer term,' he said, 'except for my exams. I've got to do well. The scholarship for the law school's at the end of May, but it'll make me work even harder knowing I've got you. And if I pass, I'll have to leave in September, to go to university, but I'll be back here for all the . . .'

'Leave?' said Hannah. 'You're going away to university?'

Sami smiled down at her, his eyes wide with tenderness.

'Yes, but it won't affect us. We'll write. And I'll be back every holiday. Just think, this place will be waiting for us. It'll be in my mind all the time. It's like our home.'

His arm tightened around her.

'Kiss me,' he said. 'Oh Hannah, you've no idea how much I love you.'

His kiss was more confident this time and when

Hannah tried to pull away he didn't notice, but pressed his lips more firmly on hers.

She wanted him to go on and she wanted him to stop, and it was only when his hand crept up towards her breast that she found the strength to push him away.

'No!' she said, standing up. 'I've got to go now!'

His brows twitched together in a frown.

'You're not angry with me?'

She shook her head.

'We're not the same as other people.' He put his arms round her again, but so gently that she felt no need to resist. 'We're in love. We're going to get married one day and have lots of babies like Yusuf.'

'Susu, you mean.'

She couldn't help laughing, although sadness was creeping across her happiness like a shadow on the sun.

'What would be wrong for other people wouldn't be wrong for us,' Sami went on. 'We'll be lovers like the poets were, but without all the tragic endings.'

He saw the smile fade from Hannah's face and kissed her lightly on the nose.

'No no,' he said. 'You don't have to worry about the babies coming too soon. I'll take care of that. You can trust me, Hannah. You can trust me always, for the rest of your life.'

CHAPTER THIRTEEN

Hannah sat on the bus, hardly conscious of the people who were crowding into the seats nearby. She could still feel Sami's arms round her, still taste his lips on hers.

Our own special place, she thought, going over in her mind every corner of the clearing, seeing the wall where she'd sat with Sami and the place where they'd been standing for their last kiss.

'We're not like other people,' he'd said. 'We'll be lovers like the poets were.'

She'd half believed him then. She wanted to believe him now. She thought of how it would be – running to meet him in the stork garden after school, feeling her heart leap when she saw him, entering that closed protected circle of happiness time after time. And then becoming lovers, true lovers – her daydream faltered. She couldn't go on imagining it clearly.

What sort of girl does that? she thought. How do they end up?

The bus had stopped and people were getting off. Hannah noticed almost too late that this was the stop for home. She jumped up and pushed her way to the door just before it closed.

Slowly she walked down the main street, then turned down the alleyway and stood for a moment outside the door before she knocked on it.

Mrs Rasi opened it almost at once.

'Hello, love. How was it? Did you have a nice time?'

'Yes, thanks.'

Susu was playing on the floor, banging a spoon on an enamel plate and singing tunelessly.

'Were there lots of people there? Was the place crowded?'

'Not really. Hardly anyone.'

Granny came out of the next room, yawning after her afternoon nap.

'Hannah!' she said, beaming. 'You're home! Let's have tea. I want you to tell me all about it.'

Hannah turned away.

'Maybe later, Gran,' she said. 'I've – I've got a headache.'

'A headache?'

Granny raised her eyebrows anxiously towards her daughter, but Mrs Rasi shook her head.

'It can't be. The doctor said the others couldn't get it, not after that medicine they took. You haven't got a fever, have you, Hannah?'

'Oh, stop it!' Hannah burst out, unable to bear it a moment longer. 'I've had a nice afternoon and I haven't got meningitis and I just want to rest, that's all!'

She ran into the next room and flung herself down on the bed.

'Better leave her for a while,' she heard Granny say. 'She probably sat in the sun too long. Why don't you take her in a nice cup of tea a bit later on.'

'If it was those girls upsetting her again,' Mrs Rasi

said. 'I'm going to get hold of them and give them a piece of my mind. You wouldn't believe how . . .'

Hannah put the pillow over her head, trying to block out their voices.

'Leave me alone!' she muttered. 'Why can't you just leave me alone?'

She imagined how they'd look if they knew what she'd been doing. Shock, bewilderment and horror would cross their faces, and then there'd be disgust and furious shouting, and her father would beat her and . . .

She felt desolate.

'Oh Sami,' she whispered. 'I wish I was with you right now.'

But the idea of Sami was frightening, too. She remembered what he'd said about babies. She wouldn't have to worry about them coming too soon, he'd said. He'd take care of all that.

Hannah took the pillow off her head, turned over, and lay on her back, frowning at the ceiling.

He just assumes I'm going to sleep with him, she thought. He's quite sure I'll do it. What sort of girl does he think I am?

She thought of Zahra and her teasing and flirting, her tight jeans, her bangles and make-up and flicked-back hair.

At least I'm not like her, she said to herself. She began to bite a fingernail, worrying at it with her teeth. But not even Zahra would have done what I've done – gone off secretly to meet a boy, let him think we're going to be lovers . . . Does Sami respect me, or does he despise me in his heart of hearts?

She saw again in her mind's eye the tenderness in his face as he'd looked at her, and her doubts fled and she wriggled with contentment.

He's really in love with me, she thought. Really and truly. And I'm in love with him.

She lay still for a moment, savouring a rich flush of happiness. Then, from the next room, she heard her mother's voice call out something, and Granny's answering chuckle.

She sat bolt upright.

I'm mad! What have I been thinking of? I couldn't possibly sleep with a boy! I'd ruin the rest of my life!

'Hannah? What's the matter?'

Mrs Rasi was standing in the doorway, a cup of tea in her hand. 'You're too soft, love. You shouldn't let them hurt you. They're just spiteful, silly girls. You're worth ten of every one of them.'

'Oh I'm not, Mum, I'm not!'

Hannah felt like bursting into tears.

Mrs Rasi sat down on the bed and put the steaming glass into Hannah's hand.

'What did you think of that place, then? The old walled city?'

'It's lovely.' Hannah hid her face as she bent her head to take a sip of tea.

'I'm glad you've been there.' Mrs Rasi wiped her wet, worn hands on her apron. 'I wish I'd been able to take you there myself. It's a special place for you.'

Hannah looked up too fast and nearly spilled her tea. She almost said, 'How did you know?' but managed just in time to say 'What do you mean?' instead.

'Haven't you ever wondered why it took so long for you to come along after we got married?' Mrs Rasi went on. 'Seven whole years after the wedding!'

Hannah shook her head, too surprised to speak.

'I'd tried everything!' Mrs Rasi said. 'All the things you're supposed to eat and drink. Herbs, prayers, medicines. Your granny told me about the eel pond. Someone had told her about it when she came up from the country to pray for your grandad's bad eyes at Sidi Ben Daoud's tomb.'

'Told you what? I don't understand.' Hannah could hardly take in what her mother was saying.

'When you don't get a baby you feed eggs to the eels in the pond.' Mrs Rasi looked a little embarrassed. 'Oh, I know I'm always laughing at Granny for being superstitious, but I was getting desperate. And it worked, Hannah! It worked! Ten months later, you were born!'

'What?' said Hannah. 'It can't have been because of that!'

'Well –' Mrs Rasi laughed and shook her head from side to side. 'It might have been because we moved into our own house at last and had a bit of time to ourselves. We'd lived with your dad's parents up till then. But anyway, that place has something special about it. You must have felt it!'

Hannah looked at her mother as if she'd never

seen her before. In her ears were the blue glass earrings Dad had given her when he'd got his new job, and on the bridge of her nose was a scar where she'd cut herself once, running to pick up Karim when he'd fallen over. Hannah had never before noticed the lines that were appearing round her eyes and the grey hairs mixed in with the black ones.

She'd give her life for every one of us, she thought.

She bent her head to her glass, not wanting to meet her mother's searching look.

I'll lose him, she thought. If I won't be his lover he won't want to see me any more.

The sadness she'd momentarily felt in the stork garden gripped her so strongly she was afraid it would suffocate her, but under it was a small budding shoot of something else – pride, respect, knowledge of the world.

She drained the tea glass and handed it back to her mother.

'My headache's a bit better. It must have been a touch of the sun. I just need to sleep.'

Mrs Rasi nodded.

'Best thing for you. I'll wake you up at supper time.'

The door clicked shut behind her and Hannah turned her face to the wall as the tears which had gathered in her eyes began to spill down her cheeks.

CHAPTER FOURTEEN

Zahra was already at the bus stop talking to Muna and Fatima when Hannah arrived next morning.

'Here she is,' she heard Muna say. 'Don't let her get near me. I don't want to catch it.'

Zahra edged away as Hannah came up to her.

'How's your brother, then?' she said. 'Is he OK?'

'Yes, he's fine,' said Hannah, surprised. 'He's still a bit tired but that's only because he had such a high temperature.'

'You should have told me it was meningitis!' said Zahra, frowning. 'I only found out when I went to the Golden Grocery last night. I might have caught it off you.'

Hannah noticed for the first time how Zahra's mouth twisted when she talked.

'I didn't want to scare you,' she said. 'There's no danger at all from me. I've been inoculated.'

'Oh, well, that's all right then.' Zahra had begun to find the subject boring. She turned round and looked over her shoulder at Hannah. 'Well? What do you think?'

'What do I think of what?'

Hannah was looking up the street at the bus which was lumbering towards them. How am I going to get through today? she thought. How am I going to tell him?

'My jeans, of course!'

Zahra had turned back and was waiting for Hannah's compliments.

'Aren't they a bit – well, tight?' said Hannah. 'I mean, how do you sit down?'

Zahra stared at her for a moment and her eyes were blank. Then she tossed her head.

'We're very prim and proper all of a sudden, aren't we?' she said.

'No.' Hannah discovered that she didn't care

about Zahra or her jeans. 'They look a bit uncomfort-able, that's all.'

The bus pulled up and they crowded into it. Hannah took a seat near the front. The three others pushed their way to the back.

He'll be waiting for me in our secret place after school, Hannah thought, and unhappiness churned in her stomach. I'll have to go and tell him that I won't meet him there any more.

She heard rustlings from behind as the girls shared out a candy bar.

I can't face him! she thought. He'll try to persuade me again. He'll kiss me and I won't want to stop him. He might be angry even. I couldn't bear it!

Her schoolbag was on the seat beside her. She shifted it on to her knee to let an old man sit down and heard her pencils rattle in her pencil case.

A letter! she thought. I'll write him a letter!

'Are you coming, then?' said Zahra as they went out through the gates at the end of the school day.

Hannah shook her head.

'I can't. Sorry. I've got to do a bit of shopping.'

'Suit yourself. I can't say I'm surprised.'

There was an edge to Zahra's voice. Hannah turned her head to look at her.

'Why? What do you mean?'

'Not your sort of thing, really, is it, having a bit of fun? Think you're too good for us, don't you?'

'No.' Hannah looked bewildered. 'Why should I think . . .'

'Oh, don't worry about it!' Zahra turned away and beckoned to Muna who was walking out of the school entrance behind them. 'I don't care if you come anyway. Quite frankly, I don't want to go round with you any more.'

She linked her arm in Muna's and they walked off. Hannah stood still. The spite in Zahra's voice had hit her like a punch. The crowd of girls hurried past her.

'Here,' someone said behind her. 'You dropped this.'

Hannah turned round. A girl was holding out a folded piece of paper. Hannah almost snatched it from her. It was her letter to Sami! She'd been secretly writing it and rewriting it during every lesson all day. How could she have dropped it like that? Supposing someone had read it?

But the girl was looking sympathetically at her.

'You look a bit upset,' she said. 'Was that Zahra talking to you? Was she being horrible?'

Hannah nodded.

'It was nothing, really,' she said. 'It was just that . . .'

'You don't have to tell *me*.' The girl hitched her bag up on to her shoulder. 'Zahra was horrible to me when I first came to this school. Nobody likes her.'

'But I thought – I mean, she seems so popular,' Hannah said.

'Not really. People are just scared of offending her because she gets so nasty.' The girl hesitated. 'Are you going towards the bus stop? Do you want to go with me?'

Hannah smiled back at her.

'I do usually, but I've got to go and – I've got to do some shopping today. But I'd like to go with you tomorrow. I really would.'

'Great,' the girl said, and Hannah noticed how

warm and friendly her brown eyes were. 'I'll see you tomorrow, then.'

Hannah walked off quickly towards the main shopping street. She had to buy an envelope for her letter. That was easy. Then she had to deliver it. That would be more difficult. She had a plan, but she was afraid it wouldn't work.

Sami had once mentioned the place where his uncle worked. It was a dry cleaner's – something like Expert Cleaning, or Excel Cleaners. She'd have to find the place, pluck up all her courage, and ask his uncle to pass the letter on.

She bought a packet of envelopes at a corner kiosk and stood in the street, reading her letter through one last time.

Dear Sami, she had written. *I didn't know how to tell you this face to face so I'm writing you a letter instead. I understand now that I can't go on meeting you secretly. It makes me scared even to think about what would happen if my mum and dad found out and anyway, I don't feel it's right, even though I love you. Also, I know I wouldn't respect myself if we were lovers and deceiving everyone and I might regret it for the rest of my life.*

I'll never stop loving you, ever. I'm so scared that when you read this you won't love me any more. One day, when we're older, maybe it'll all come right.

Your loving

Hannah

It's not quite how I feel, she thought, but I can't say it any better, and she pulled an envelope from the packet, pushed the letter into it and sealed it.

She'd remembered seeing two or three dry cleaning places on the corner near the station and she hurried down the street towards them. The first she came to was called World Wide Services, and she walked past it. She felt sure now that she'd never find the right one. She nearly missed the second place. It was a very small shop, its narrow frontage sandwiched between a café and a food store. The sign above the door read Expert Cleaners.

Her palms were clammy with nervous sweat but she steeled herself and pushed the door open. A middle-aged man was sitting behind the counter, writing in a ledger. He looked at Hannah over his glasses.

'Yes?'

She swallowed.

'I – I've got a message for Sami.' His brows went up in surprise, but she had her story ready and hurried on. 'My brother asked me to drop it in for him. He's in Sami's class at school. Something about a book he said he'd lend him.'

The man had begun to lose interest. His eyes had gone back to his ledger.

'You are – Sami's uncle, aren't you?' Hannah said timidly.

The man didn't bother to look up again.

'Yes. Put it down here. I'll see he gets it.'

Hannah dropped the letter on the counter and gave it one last anxious look. It lay innocently among the bills and laundry dockets as if it didn't, after all, hold the key to everything that mattered in the world.

'Thank you,' she whispered, and suddenly realizing that Sami himself might come home at any minute, she ran back to the door and fled from the shop.

CHAPTER FIFTEEN

For the next few days Hannah could think of nothing but her letter. Had Sami ever got it? Had it made him very unhappy? Perhaps he was angry and bitter. Perhaps she'd made him lose faith in love and poetry and even life itself.

She felt sure at first that somehow he would try to answer it, to see her again and persuade her that she was wrong. She both longed to meet him again and was frightened at the same time. He was with her every minute of the day, a glorious presence in her mind, and if she saw him again in reality she was afraid her good resolutions would melt away. She was afraid that she'd creep back into that blissful place where only the two of them existed and the rest of the world and its rules and punishments seemed a long way away.

She was worried at first that he'd try to reach her through Zahra, who would now barely speak to her, and stared through her with cold hostility whenever they met at the bus stop or passed in the school corridor. If Sami gave Zahra a letter to pass to her, Zahra would open it and read it out to the others, spread rumours, laugh in corners . . .

Hannah watched Zahra anxiously, but she showed no sign of holding any secret knowledge.

The school gate was the only other place where Sami might contact her and every day Hannah looked round anxiously, both dreading and yearning for the sight of his eager face and tousled thatch of hair.

Her new friend, Zabidah, always walked to the bus stop with her now. Hannah liked Zabidah more than any other girl she'd met at school and they were quickly becoming friends, but she felt uneasy every day as she walked through the big metal gates in case Sami was there, watching out for her, deciding not to approach her if she was talking to someone else.

She needn't have worried. A week passed and then another but Sami didn't come. Several times she thought she saw him. Her heart bumped painfully and a dizzy feeling came over her but then the person would turn round or she'd look again and see that it wasn't him.

After four weeks, Hannah had almost given up hope of ever seeing Sami again. She still thought about him all the time but her feelings kept changing. Sometimes she was sunk in a kind of settled sadness, feeling that beauty and richness had gone from life, leaving a dull dreariness behind. At other times she was angry.

I'm stupid! Stupid! she'd mutter angrily to herself. Why was I always so quiet and shy? If I'd had any brains at all I'd have been able to tell him I wouldn't make love but I might have been able to keep him as my friend. Now I've lost him altogether.

Sometimes she was angry with Sami.

He shouldn't have tried to do things with me, she thought, more and more often. He knows what would have happened if I'd been found out, or had a baby.

The very idea of it convulsed her in a shudder.

And then, one day, she met him. It was quite by chance. She was sitting in the bus on the way home from school, looking out of the window, wondering why the streets looked so dull and cheerless in the bright summer sunshine. She didn't see him until he dropped into the seat beside her.

'Hannah,' he said.

She turned her head and gasped. She felt almost faint and knew she was trembling.

'You never came back!' he said. 'I waited hours for you, every day!'

Hannah had to clear her throat before she could speak.

'Didn't you get my letter?'

'Yes, but not for two weeks! I found it on the counter in my uncle's shop by accident, under a pile of . . .'

'I'm sorry,' said Hannah. 'He promised he'd give it to you. I wrote it the day after – the day after we met that time.'

'You hardly wrote anything! Just a little note, saying you didn't want to see me any more!'

'I didn't say that,' Hannah said timidly. 'I just said I couldn't meet you secretly and it wouldn't be right to . . .'

'If only you'd come back to our special place and talked to me properly!'

'I couldn't have said it out loud.' Hannah's feeling of shock was subsiding now. She was becoming used to him sitting beside her and she found she could speak more easily. 'I was afraid you'd try to . . . I was afraid you wouldn't listen.'

He was about to take her hand but an old woman in the seat on the far side of the aisle was looking at them curiously, so he dropped his hand back on to his knee and lowered his voice to a whisper.

'Not listen? Of course I'd have listened! You were my whole life!'

She noticed that he'd said 'were' instead of 'are' and bent her head, pain running through her like poison.

'Why didn't you come and find me before?' she whispered at last, lifting her head to his. 'I wanted to go on being friends.'

'I've had my exams. I couldn't think about anything else.'

She felt another stab of pain.

'Oh? Did they go all right?'

She wanted more than anything else to keep her dignity, not to let him see how badly she wanted to cry.

'Yes! Very well! I've got my scholarship, in fact. I'm going off to Law School in September.'

'That's great. Congratulations.'

He didn't notice the formality in her voice. He was speaking again, a little too loudly, and she looked anxiously towards the woman in the far seat, hoping she couldn't hear.

'Anyway, I'm free for the next few months,' he said. 'I'm going home to see my parents, but only for a while. Then I'll be back for the rest of the summer. My uncle's given me a job in his laundry, so I can save up for next term. We'll go to the stork garden as often as we like! No, don't worry. I won't make you do anything you don't want. We'll just talk, and I'll tell you all my plans . . .'

She felt that she'd never really known him, and that he'd never understood her at all.

'Maybe,' she said, standing up. 'This is my stop. I've got to get off here.'

He stood to let her pass and her hand brushed his. She felt its warmth but nothing more.

She smiled at him. She didn't want to cry now. She felt strong and free.

'Goodbye, Sami,' she said.

He squeezed her arm.

'Goodbye for now. I'll see you again soon. When I get back. We'll . . .'

She turned and smiled at him one last time as she stepped off the bus. It rumbled away, its old engine roaring as it began to climb the hill. She watched it go.

Then she heard a noise in the sky and looked up. A stork was flying overhead, soaring on still wings from the direction of the stork garden. It settled on the highest frond of a palm at the edge of the road, laid its neck down along its back and began to clatter loudly with its beak.

'Not here,' it seemed to say. 'Not now. Not yet.'